JEAN E. PENDZIWOL

Pictures by
ISABELLE ARSENAULT

GROUNDWOOD BOOKS   HOUSE OF ANANSI PRESS   TORONTO   BERKELEY

Once upon
a northern
night

ONCE UPON a northern night
while you lay sleeping,
wrapped in a downy blanket,
I painted you a picture.

It started with one tiny flake,
perfect
and beautiful
and special,
just like you.
Then there were two,
and then three.

Soon
the night sky filled with
sparkling specks of white,
crowding
and floating,
tumbling down to the welcoming
ground
until the earth was
wrapped in a downy blanket,
just like you.

Once upon a northern night
pine trees held out prickly hands
to catch the falling flakes
that gathered into puffs of creamy white,
settling like balls of cotton,
waiting.

When you walk beneath the trees
the wind will tickle them
until they drop their snowy treasures,
dusting your hair and
sprinkling your nose.

Once upon a northern night
a mother deer led her fawn
around the silent birch
and traced
a wandering path
on my canvas of white.

They nuzzled the sleeping garden
with memories of summer,
then wandered off
to taste the frozen fruit
still clinging to an apple tree.

Once upon a northern night
a great gray owl gazed down
with his great yellow eyes
on the milky-white bowl of your yard.

Without a sound,
not even the quietest whisper,
his great silent wings lifted and
down,
down,
down
he drifted,
leaving a feathery sketch
of his passing
in the snow.

Once upon a northern night
two snowshoe hares
scampered and chased
as they played a nighttime game of tag.

The fox,
in his auburn coat and long black boots,
wanted to play, too.
But the hares became silent
and oh so still,
crouched beneath the winter-bare dogwood,
playing hide-and-seek
until the fox gave up
and pranced off into the darkness.

Once upon a northern night
a small,
small mouse
with big,
big ears
scurried along the deck,
searching.

Across the table,
mounded with snowy white
like vanilla ice cream,
he ran,
tunneling beneath the drifts
to a midnight feast of seeds
that lay scattered
beneath the bird feeder.

Once upon a northern night,
deep,
deep
in the darkest hours,
the snowy clouds crept away
and stars appeared —
twinkling points of light
hanging in the purple sky.

I knew by the time you woke,
the sun would have chased them away,
so I set them like diamonds
on the branches of the willow.

Once upon a northern night
melodies of
green and
pink and
orange
sang across the sky.

I tried to capture them
but they were much too nimble,
and only their rhythm reached you,
deep in slumber,
rising and falling
with each sweet,
peaceful breath.

Once upon a northern night
I sent the frost
to dance on your window
and make a frame.

It twirled and twisted,
curled and coiled,
spiraled and spun,
climbing around the edges of the glass
but leaving the middle
as smooth and clear as the frozen pond.

Once upon a northern night
while you lay sleeping,
wrapped in a downy blanket,
I painted you a picture.

And then
I had the moon gently kiss you
and the wind whisper…
I love you.

To Josiah, Katy and Alex, in loving
memory of their mother, my beautiful
sister, Theresa. — JEP

To J & M
Thank you for your inspiration and
generosity. — IA

Text copyright © 2013 by Jean E. Pendziwol
Illustrations copyright © 2013 by Isabelle Arsenault
Published in Canada and the USA in 2013 by Groundwood Books
Fourth printing 2015

Groundwood Books / House of Anansi Press
110 Spadina Avenue, Suite 801, Toronto, Ontario M5V 2K4
or c/o Publishers Group West
1700 Fourth Street, Berkeley, CA 94710

We acknowledge for their financial support of our publishing program
the Canada Council for the Arts, the Government of Canada through
the Canada Book Fund (CBF) and the Ontario Arts Council.

Canada Council   Conseil des Art
for the Arts   du Canada

ONTARIO ARTS COUNCIL
CONSEIL DES ARTS DE L'ONTARIO
an Ontario government agency
un organisme du gouvernement de l'Ontario

Library and Archives Canada Cataloguing in Publication
Pendziwol, Jean E.
Once upon a northern night / Jean E. Pendziwol ; illustrated
by Isabelle Arsenault.
ISBN 978-1-55498-138-0
I. Arsenault, Isabelle II. Title.
PS8581.E55312O64 2013   jC813'.54   C2013-900372-X

The illustrations were done in mixed media (pencil, gouache, watercolor
and ink) and assembled digitally.
Design by Michael Solomon
Printed and bound in Malaysia

FSC
www.fsc.org
MIX
Paper from
responsible sources
FSC® C012700